A SIMPLE BRO

L.J. Davis

Illustrations by Lisa Victoria

Publisher's Cataloging-in-Publication
(Provided by Quality Books, Inc.)

Davis, L. J.
A simple brown leaf / by L.J. Davis.
p. cm.
SUMMARY: An autumn leaf is caught by a squirrel who uses it to line her nest for the coming winter months.
Audience: Ages 3–7.
LCCN 2004097830
ISBN 0-9762007-8-3

1. Squirrels—Juvenile fiction. 2. Life cycles (Biology)—Juvenile fiction. [1. Squirrels—Fiction. 2. Animal life cycles—Fiction. 3. Plant life cycles—Fiction.]   I. Title.

PZ7.D29466Sim 2004   [E]
QBI04-800108

First American Edition, December 2004

Published by Abovo Publishing
Printed in the United States of America

10 9 8 7 6 5 4 3 2 1   04 05 06 07 08

For Ceiley and Dempsey

The leaf had been the color of a leathery
brown for some time now.

Once, when newly born, it was the purest color of green.

A green so sharp that it looked
like a polished emerald.

As time went by,
and the sky got bluer and the days warmer,

its tint began to mellow
into a rich

grass

green.

As more days stretched by,
    the deep dark hues
        began to fade into an uglyish yellow-green.

The leaf remained this way, looking like rot,
    for quite some time.

As the days shortened and the nights chilled,
    the simple leaf turned brown.

        It remained this color for all of autumn.

Now, as the cold of night lengthened
into the chilliness
of day,
the leaf was adrift on a confused current of air—jerking

this way   and   that way,   floating higher

then
plunging
downward,

until at last it started towards Earth.

The leaf thought it was the end, but it wasn't.
Someone was watching the simple brown leaf.

Someone had been watching the leaf for a long time.

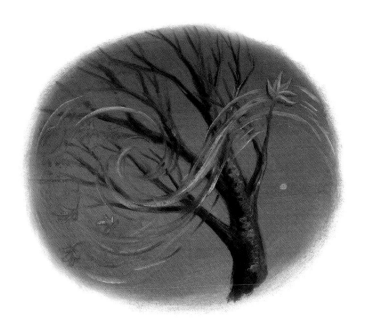

As the leaf floated gently to the ground,
a young squirrel looked up in anticipation.

She had been watching the leaf all summer.
She liked how broad and sturdy the leaf seemed
while tucked between the other leaves.

When the mighty winds shook the tree hard,
the leaf remained strong.
When all of the other leaves
frayed and crumbled
with each gust of wind,

the brown leaf stood its place.

She needed this leaf!

The squirrel knew that winter was coming and she had to prepare. Throughout the summer, on into autumn, she watched for that one special leaf to fall, so she could use it for her nest.

For animals who don't have to make nests for winter, for those who spend their cold days tucked under a warm blanket or snuggled by a cozy fire, it is hard to understand why a squirrel would be so keen about a simple brown leaf.

But, the squirrel was not one of those animals.

If the squirrel did not make a proper nest, she would freeze during the icy winter chill.

Her nest had to be warm.
It had to block out the cold.

If it didn't, she would not make it to the spring.

Before the leaf touched the ground, the squirrel sprung
up to claim it.

Treating it gently and with great care,
        she entered her tree den
        high atop a mighty oak

        and approached her nest.

She had been building this nest for quite some time,
adding bits of straw and twigs
and other brown leaves

to make it warm and cozy.

As it was, her nest would do nicely,
but she knew that she needed the special warmth
only the simple brown leaf could give.

Carefully, she placed the leaf on the top of her nest.
No longer would she worry

about the winter cold.

The leaf did not quite know what to make of this
peculiar situation. When the wind snatched it from its tree,
the leaf thought it would die.

But, it didn't feel dead.

In fact, it felt very much alive.

When it was tethered, the leaf
helped the tree survive by
gathering light and rain.

Now the leaf was helping the
squirrel survive by providing
warmth.

The leaf never realized that it could have
more than one purpose.

With this understanding,
the leaf felt transformed.
It could almost feel the green of youth
course through its veins.

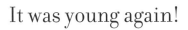

It was young again!

It was vibrant!

It continued to have a purpose!

Outside,
the chilly wind flung itself furiously against the tree.
No leaves lingered on the ground. Creatures scurried
to and fro, gathering one last nut, one last meal,
before escaping into their dens.

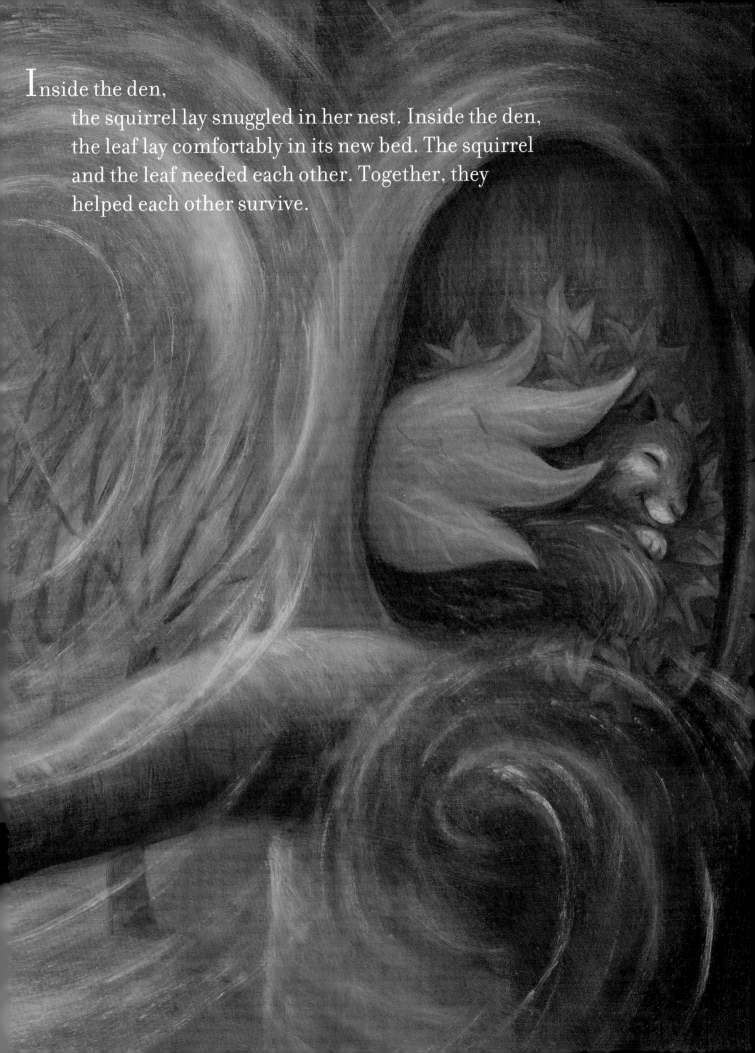

Inside the den,
the squirrel lay snuggled in her nest. Inside the den,
the leaf lay comfortably in its new bed. The squirrel
and the leaf needed each other. Together, they
helped each other survive.

All creatures need each other to survive.
All creatures give each other purpose.

Even animals that spend their cold days tucked under
a warm blanket or snuggled by a cozy fire are needed
to do special things.

You are meant to do something wonderful!

Someone loves you!

Someone needs you...
just like the squirrel needed the simple brown leaf.

The author welcomes your comments at:

ljdavis.com